Heifer International
1 World Avenue, Little Rock, AR, 72202
United States
www.heifer.org

Sometimes simple concepts are the most
profound. The concept of Heifer International
— give people a means to raise themselves
up out of poverty and then ask them to pass
it on— is simple, but profoundly effective.
Since 1944, Heifer has helped more than
9.2 million families in more than 125 countries
move toward greater self-reliance through gifts
of livestock and training in environmentally
sound agriculture. The impact of each initial
gift is multiplied as recipients agree to "pass on
the gift" by giving one or more of their animal's
offspring or the equivalent to another in need.
Visit Heifer.org to learn more about ways your
family can help end hunger and poverty.

Once There Was and Was Not:
A Modern Day Folktale from Armenia

Text copyright © 2008 by Page McBrier

Illustrations copyright © 2008 by Stefano Vitale

Designed and produced by
  Verve Marketing & Design,
  Chadds Ford, PA 19317 USA

Printed on 10% post-consumer paper, using
lead-free, soy ink: 20% soy or vegetable content.

Text is set in Locarno.

Printed in the U.S.A

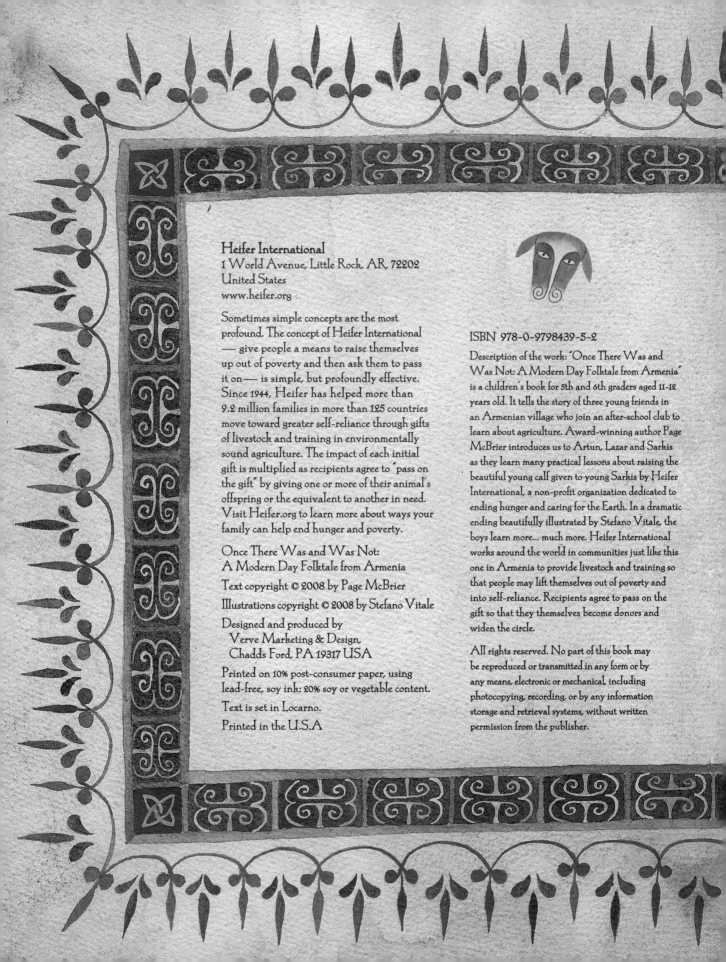

ISBN 978-0-9798439-5-2

Description of the work: "Once There Was and
Was Not: A Modern Day Folktale from Armenia"
is a children's book for 5th and 6th graders aged 11-12
years old. It tells the story of three young friends in
an Armenian village who join an after-school club to
learn about agriculture. Award-winning author Page
McBrier introduces us to Artun, Lazar and Sarkis
as they learn many practical lessons about raising the
beautiful young calf given to young Sarkis by Heifer
International, a non-profit organization dedicated to
ending hunger and caring for the Earth. In a dramatic
ending beautifully illustrated by Stefano Vitale, the
boys learn more... much more. Heifer International
works around the world in communities just like this
one in Armenia to provide livestock and training so
that people may lift themselves out of poverty and
into self-reliance. Recipients agree to pass on the
gift so that they themselves become donors and
widen the circle.

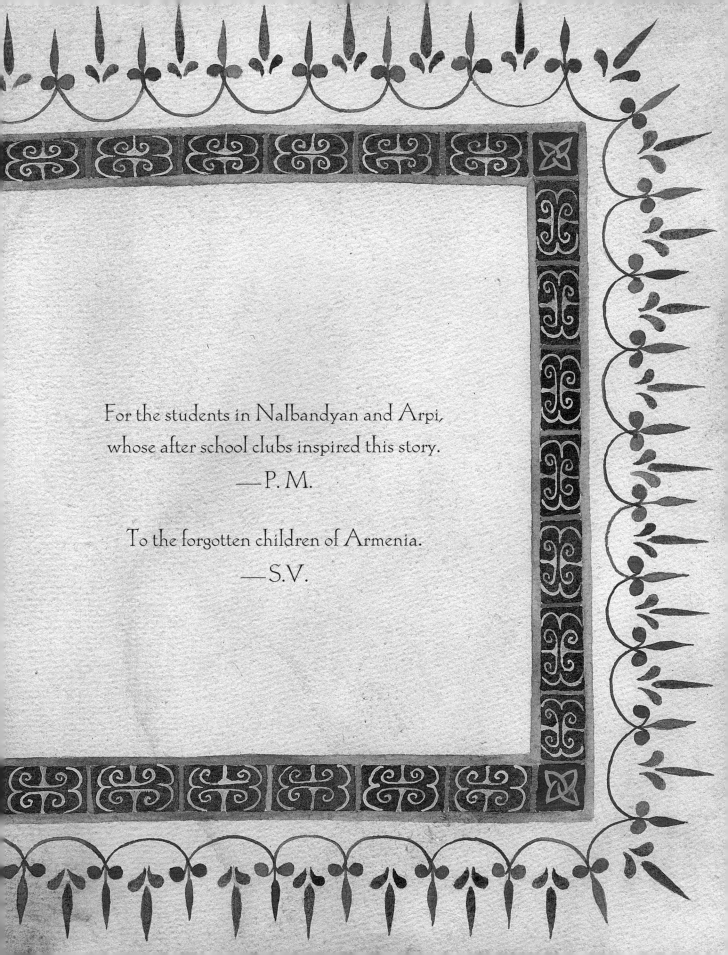

For the students in Nalbandyan and Arpi,
whose after school clubs inspired this story.

—P. M.

To the forgotten children of Armenia.

—S. V.

Heifer
INTERNATIONAL

www.heifer.org

ONCE

THERE WAS AND WAS NOT

A Modern Day Folktale
from Armenia

By PAGE McBRIER
Illustrated By STEFANO VITALE

nce there was and was not in modern Armenia a boy named Artun. He lived on a farm in a small village with a big name. Now because there were few jobs in Nalbandyan, Artun's family had no steady income, and survived instead on whatever they managed to grow on their meager patch of land.

One day, as Artun helped his
mother pick apples, he said, "If only
we had a cow, we could have yogurt
and cheese for supper tonight."

"Artun!" his mother said. "Wish
for a cow for your neighbor instead,
that good fortune may give you two.
You should never envy others."

So Artun, who was mostly obedient,
did exactly that.

Now not long after, something new and exciting happened at school. The headmaster called everyone together and said, "Beginning next week, we will offer six after school clubs to anyone interested." He described each club, and the kinds of things the students would be doing.

On the way home, Artun and his two friends, Sarkis and Lazar, tried to decide. "How about ecology?" suggested Artun.

"No, journalism," offered Lazar.

"I think we should sign up for agriculture," Sarkis announced. "We'll learn how to care for calves."

Artun and Lazar burst out laughing. "We have no calves," Lazar pointed out.

Sarkis shrugged. "Maybe some day."

Artun and Lazar doubted it, but because Sarkis signed up and they were such good friends, they did, too.

Throughout the fall, the club met every week and…what do you know? They had a lot of fun.

In the last week of October — following a skit on how to bathe a calf that starred Artun as the uncooperative calf — the teacher made an announcement. "Next week, the class will receive a gift."

No one — including Artun — paid much attention, figuring it was probably something like a plaque with the club motto. Imagine their astonishment, then, when they were led outside to a grassy patch where a cluster of baby calves mewed and tugged on their leads.

The class stood speechless as the teacher announced, "A generous donor has provided us with 10 dairy calves."

11

Ten? Wait a minute. As everyone cheered, Artun quickly counted 15 club members. What about the others?

The teacher held up a small bag. "Please choose a slip of paper. If your paper has an X, you may pick out a calf."

Artun, Lazar and Sarkis opened theirs together. "X," shouted Sarkis, just as Artun saw that his and Lazar's were blank.

His shoulders slumped. How could this be? He glanced at Lazar, who looked equally miserable, and then he remembered his mother's warning. "Congratulations," he said with a grin, punching Sarkis' arm.

"Yes," added Lazar, punching the other arm.

"Ow, thanks," said Sarkis. For a moment, he grew quiet. "You know what? We can take care of her together."

"Are you sure?" Artun asked.

"Of course."

And so Sarkis gathered one of the baby calves in his arms, and the three of them, taking turns carrying their bundle of good fortune, whooped and hollered all the way to Sarkis' house.

That afternoon, the boys built a stall in one corner of the shed. Artun helped Lazar pencil in the first notation in the new log book: the name of the calf and how much food and water she'd had that day.

As her name suggested, *Maral, Beautiful,* was indeed lovely,
and although she didn't belong to Artun or Lazar, she acted
as though they were important by always coming right up to them.

As autumn faded, Artun brought Maral apple cores and
brushed her thickening coat. When she cried for her mother,
he whispered songs and stroked her neck.

Now that they had a real calf, the lessons learned in the club were put to practice. When the cold winter weather arrived, Artun mucked the stall as Lazar and Sarkis scrubbed the trough and pail with hot water. Together, the boys led her on her first walk in the snow, laughing as she gingerly stepped through the snowflakes.

Every once in a while, Artun caught himself wishing Maral were his, but quickly pushed the thought away.

Maral grew like a vine. By spring, she was as tall as Artun. Sometimes the boys would take her to the field and tie her up while they played soccer. On Sunday afternoons, Artun led her down the road and back to visit another classmate's calf.

As May approached, the Agriculture Club planned its big event: an Animal Fair. Each calf was to be judged in five categories, and the boys kept busy preparing Maral and organizing for the fair.

The day finally arrived. Family and friends had been invited, and as the crowd grew and folk music filled the air, Lazar and Artun waited for Sarkis. At the judging table, the visiting judges put on long, white lab coats. The mayor arrived and took his place behind the table.

Sarkis and Maral were nowhere to be found. Then finally, Artun spotted Sarkis' father hurrying towards them with Maral. "Sarkis is very sick. We've taken him to the hospital."

The boys gasped. The hospital? Lately, Sarkis had looked a little pale and tired, but this was unexpected. Artun felt speechless with sadness.

Sarkis' father tried to reassure them, to let them know Sarkis would be all right. "He'll be home from the hospital the day after tomorrow," he said.

"But what about the Fair?" Lazar asked. "What's going to happen to Maral?"

Sarkis' father pressed the log book into Lazar's hands and said, "Lazar, I'd like for you to show Maral today."

Now it was Lazar's turn to be surprised. "Me? No...I..." For weeks, Sarkis had practiced for the Fair, and cleaned and brushed Maral's coat until it shined. Yes, of course Artun and Lazar had helped, but no one knew Maral like Sarkis.

For one small moment, Artun wished it were him, but quickly said, "You can do this, Lazar. I'll help you put on her decorations."

Right away they got to work. Maral wouldn't stand still, and kept looking around for Sarkis. "Shh, shh," whispered Artun. Just as they attached the final garland, the mayor announced the start of the contest.

As Lazar led Maral to her place in the ring, Artun found a spot on the edge of the crowded circle. "Good luck," he called.

Each person introduced his animal. In a wobbly voice, Lazar said, "This is Maral, and I am Lazar. Maral is as beautiful as her name, except when she was small and didn't like to be bathed." When the crowd laughed, Lazar relaxed.

After the introductions, the animals were measured, weighed, examined, poked and prodded. The random questions came next. When Lazar read his aloud, "How do you feed a 3 month old calf?" Artun sighed with relief. Easy. The final criteria, judging the log books, didn't worry Artun much either, since he knew they'd kept good records, even pasting in a few photos of Maral as she grew.

While the judges tallied the scores, the calves and their owners waited anxiously in the circle, chatting with bystanders and soothing their animals.

Finally, the judges approached the microphone and announced the winners. "Fourth place, Julietta. Third place, Anna. Second..." As the winners came up to receive their prizes, Artun kept glancing at Lazar and Maral. They'd worked so hard.

"First place, Lazar," the judge announced.

The audience burst into cheers as Lazar stepped forward to receive his prize: a camera and a new notebook.

Artun rushed up. "Sarkis will be so proud."

Behind them, the judges had huddled together again, and the next thing Artun knew, they pushed forward and quieted the crowd.

"Ladies and gentlemen," one of the judges boomed. "We've just learned that the young man who showed the winning calf was not its owner. Our good thoughts are with Sarkis for a speedy recovery."

The judge beamed at Lazar. "This boy," she said, "wasn't lucky enough to get a calf, but instead of dropping out, he remained committed to the club." Now she paused. "The judges are so impressed that this boy managed to win first place that we've pledged to somehow find the funding to give him a calf."

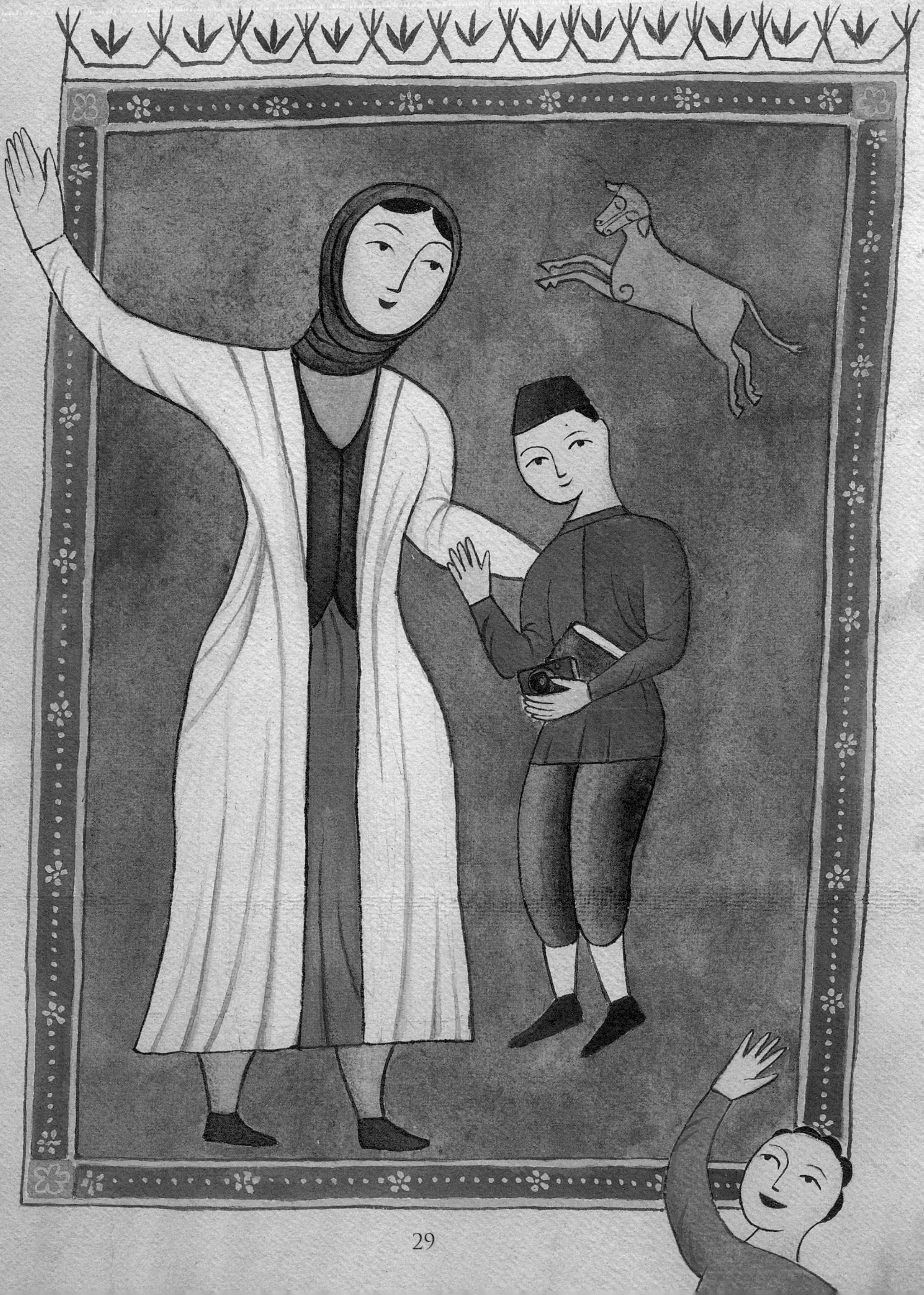

The crowd erupted in bravos and applause, and Artun, cheering the loudest, almost missed the next sentence. "And there's another boy who did the same. Artun, we'd like to give you a calf as well, for all your hard work and commitment."

And so it was that when Artun wished for a cow for his neighbor, he was given two, and no longer had to dream about yogurt and cheese.

And thus he achieved his heart's desire, and so, one day, may you.

The End